FRIENDS
OF ACPL

P9-CDB-798

SIMON & SCHUSTER PROUDLY PRESENTS

O COME, ALL YE FAITHFUL

PERFORMED BY YE BETHLEHEM ALL·STARS

penned·by·David Christiana

Simon & Schuster Books for Young Readers
NEW YORK LONDON TORONTO SYDNEY SINGAPORE

SIMON & SCHUSTER BOOKS FOR YOUNG READERS
An imprint of Simon & Schuster Children's Publishing Division
1230 Avenue of the Americas, New York, New York 10020
Illustrations copyright © 2003 by David Christiana
SIMON & SCHUSTER BOOKS FOR YOUNG READERS is a trademark of Simon & Schuster.
Book design by Greg Stadnyk
The text of this book is hand-drawn by the illustrator and typeset in Catull.
The illustrations are rendered in watercolor and gouache.
Manufactured in China
2 4 6 8 10 9 7 5 3 1
Library of Congress Cataloging-in-Publication Data
Wade, John Francis, 1711 or 12-1786. [Adeste fideles. Text. English]
O come all ye faithful / illustrated by David Christiana.— 1st ed. p. cm.Summary:
Illustrated version of the familiar Christmas carol in which the stabled animals
watch over their young as Joseph and the Virgin Mary watch over the Baby Jesus.
ISBN 0-689-85967-8 (N/A) 1. Carols, English–Texts. [1. Carols, English.
2. Christmas music. 3. Jesus Christ–Nativity.] I. Christiana, David, ill. II. Title.
BV469.W34 A3413 2003   782.28'1723–dc21   2002155723

first edition

To Skeeto
—D. C.

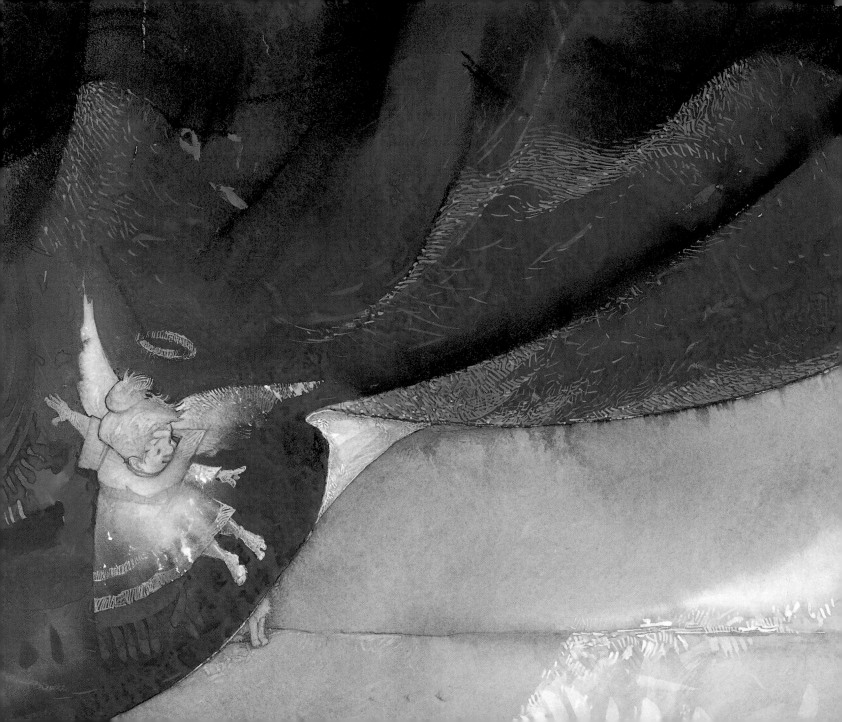

triumphant

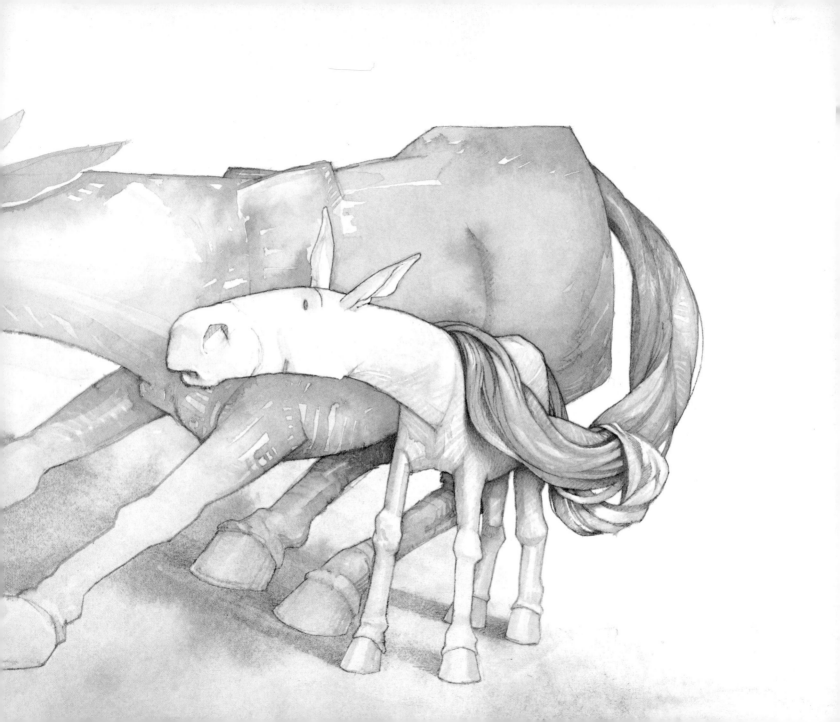

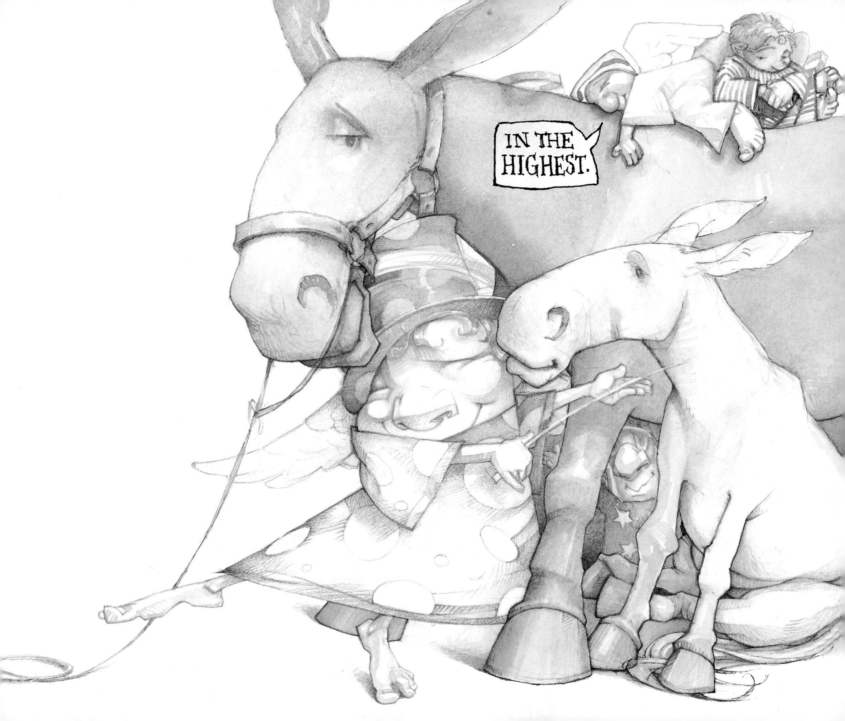

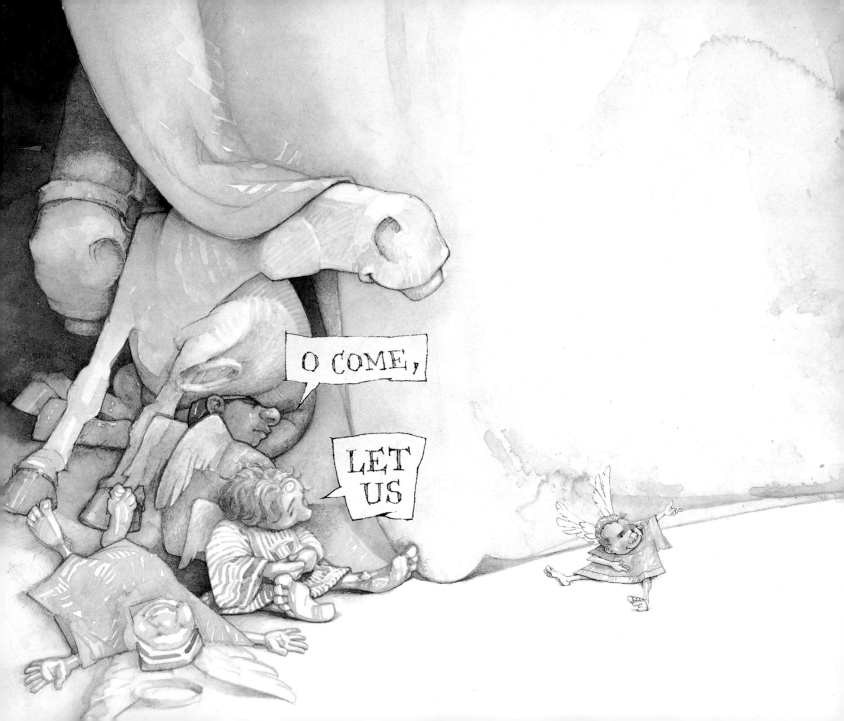

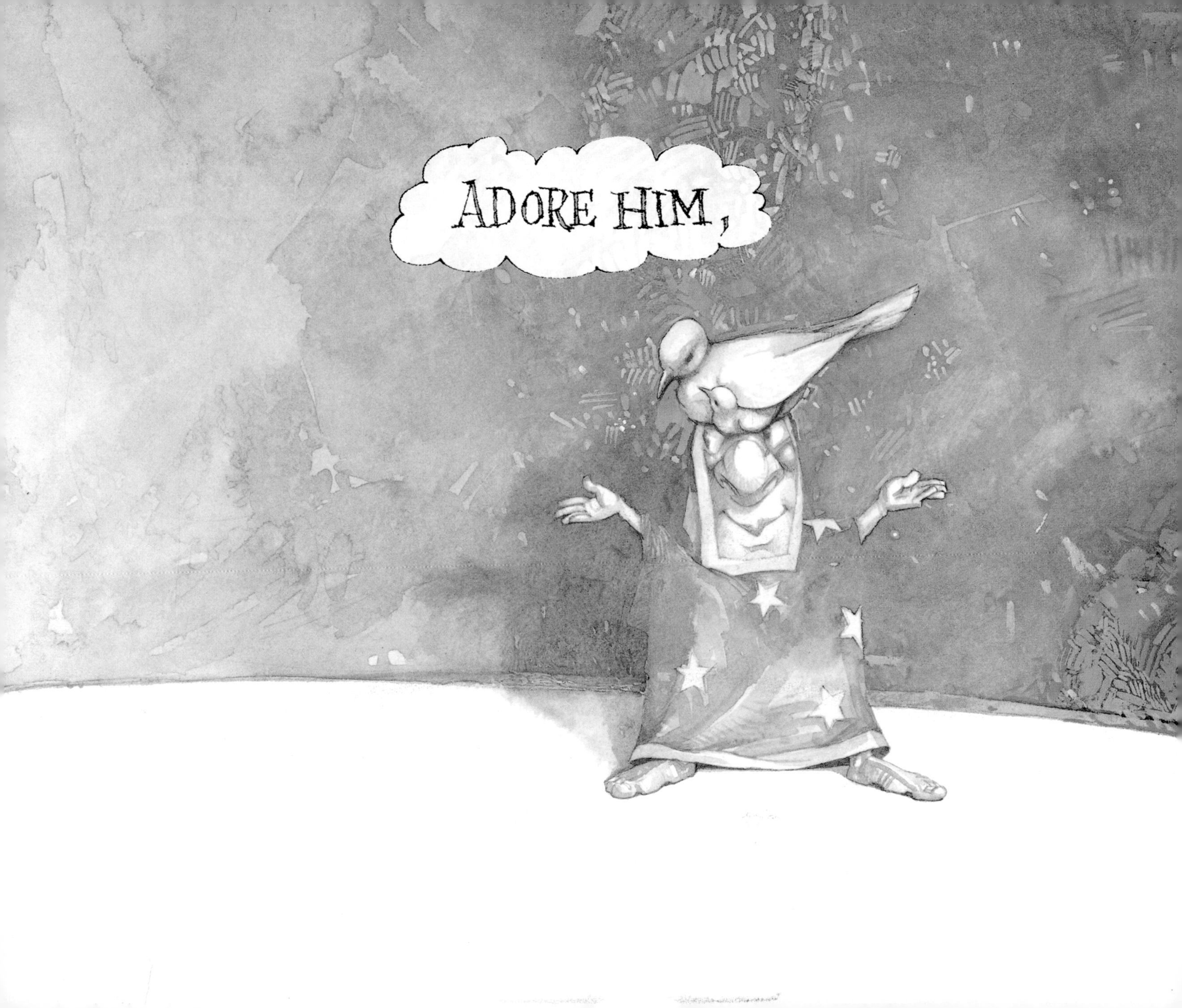
ADORE HIM,

ADORE HiM,

O COME, ALL YE FAITHFUL

Original Latin text by John Francis Wade, translated by Frederick Oakley
Music by John Francis Wade*

*While it is generally accepted that exiled Englishman John Francis Wade (c. 1711–1786) wrote the Latin text for "Adeste Fideles" in approximately 1743 and that clergyman Frederick Oakley (1802–1880) translated the included verses–which are the first and third of six–in 1841, some music historians attribute the music to John Reading (c. 1686–1764).